WILLIAM
& THE MISSING
MASTERPIECE

For Kate, for all the help and cake along the way

First U.S. edition 2015

Library of Congress Catalog Card Number 2014939359
ISBN 978-0-7636-7596-7

14 15 16 17 18 19 TLF 10 9 8 7 6 5 4 3 2 1

Printed in Dongguan, Guandong, China

This book was typeset in Times New Roman.
The illustrations were done in pencil and gouache.

TEMPLAR BOOKS

an imprint of
Candlewick Press
99 Dover Street
Somerville, Massachusetts 02144
www.candlewick.com

HELEN HANCOCKS

WILLIAM
& THE MISSING
MASTERPIECE

templar books

an imprint of Candlewick Press

William, international cat of mystery, was planning a vacation when he was interrupted by a telephone call.

On the line was Monsieur Gruyère, from a museum in Paris.

"A terrible thing has happened!" he shouted. "Our most famous painting, the *Mona Cheesa,* has been stolen!"

STOLEN!

"The timing couldn't be worse! It's National Cheese Week,
and my museum had planned to hold an exhibit in its honor.
William, can you help us find the missing masterpiece?"

William agreed at once to help and began packing his bags.
His vacation would have to wait.

Soon William was in Paris,
the city of art and cheese.

HOMAGE TO FROMAGE
GALA

CHEESE FESTIVAL

He headed to the museum to get to work on the case.

William arrived at
the scene of the crime.
Monsieur Gruyère showed him
the museum's fine paintings, and the
gap where the *Mona Cheesa* used to hang.

une fromage.

"No suspects were seen," he said,
"and no evidence has been found!
I fear we have lost the *Mona Cheesa* forever!"
It seemed that William had his work cut out for him.

William examined the room. At first, there didn't seem to be much evidence.

On closer inspection, however, William found

a small hole in the baseboard

and a strand of red yarn.

This was all very perplexing.
William decided to call on two
of his artist-friends, Fifi Le Brie
and Henri Roquefort, to see if they
had any bright ideas.

Alas, Fifi and Henri couldn't help.

"We have been busy preparing for a painting competition, which opens tonight at the museum," said Henri.

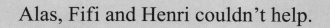

"Do come
and see if we win,"
said Fifi.

THE MINISTRY OF CHEESE
CORDIALLY INVITES
YOU TO THE

HOMAGE TO FROMAGE
ANNUAL ART GALA

A TROPHY AND A YEAR'S SUPPLY OF CHEESE FOR THE WINNER!

William decided to go. Perhaps somebody at the event would have some information about the missing masterpiece. Meanwhile, he had all afternoon to ponder the case.

But first it was time for lunch. He set off for his favorite café.

Comté — Brie — Camembert — Roquefort — Chèvre

-311-

Homage à fromage

William was just taking a digestive pause from his meal
when an unusual character caught his eye.

The shady figure was wearing a hat and a bright-red wool scarf
(which seemed strange on such a sunny day) and was carrying
a large package.

William decided to see what he was up to.

William used one of his best disguises to make sure
he stayed hidden while he kept an eye on things.

He watched the shady figure enter a costume store,
then leave with another mysterious package.

He sneakily followed the shady figure down the street,

through the park,

and over the bridge.

But before William could find out where he was going . . .

he lost him in the traffic.
How frustrating!

Suddenly, William realized
that he was late for Henri
Roquefort and Fifi
Le Brie's event.

Luckily, he saw that the
museum was just across the street.

He headed straight inside.
He would continue his investigations tomorrow.

Inside, William met Monsieur Gruyère, who was judging the competition, and his friends Henri and Fifi.

They showed William their paintings and explained that quite a stir had been made by a surprise last-minute entry.

"It is a wonderful painting!" said Monsieur Gruyère.
"But nobody has heard of this artist before."

William stared hard at the new painting.
Something about it seemed very familiar. . . .

There had been the yarn,

William thought back over his day and began to piece together the clues.

the hole in the baseboard,

the shady figure carrying a large package,

the costume store,

the mysterious painting,

and the prize, a year's supply of —

"CHEESE!"

William
exclaimed.

Monsieur Gruyère was just about to announce that the mystery
painter had won the competition when William stepped forward.

"Wait!" he shouted. "This artist is a fraud!" And with that, he peeled off the painting's cunning disguise to reveal . . .

the *Mona Cheesa*!

The crowd gasped in surprise.

"Stop that man!" William ordered as he suddenly spotted the shady figure in the audience, trying to make a getaway.

William tugged at the shady figure's red wool scarf, and the mystery of the missing masterpiece finally unraveled.

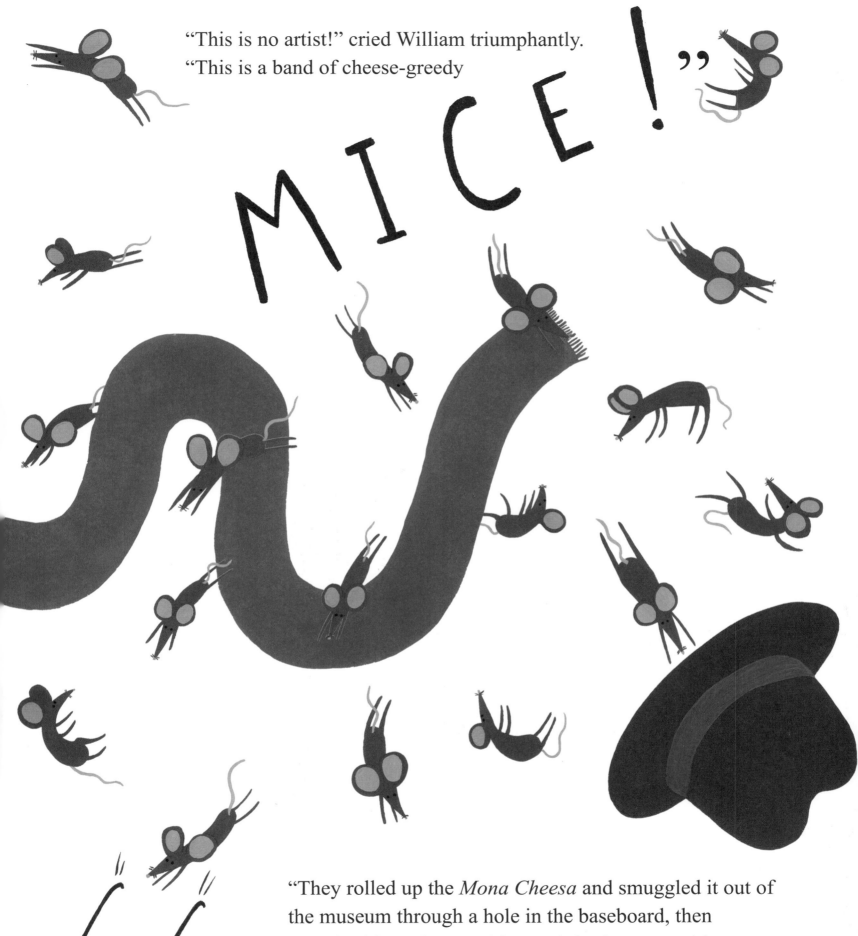

"This is no artist!" cried William triumphantly.
"This is a band of cheese-greedy

MICE!"

"They rolled up the *Mona Cheesa* and smuggled it out of the museum through a hole in the baseboard, then disguised it so they could enter it in the competition— and win a year's supply of cheese!"

Everybody was delighted with William's discovery:

Monsieur Gruyère had the *Mona Cheesa* back.

Fifi Le Brie and Henri Roquefort won
joint first prize at the Homage to Fromage.

And William could finally take his
much-deserved vacation!

POLICE ON HUNT TO TRAP PICTURE-PINCHING MICE

"No Roquefort will be left unturned!" vowed police as a nationwide search to catch the band of villainous mice got under way.

The robbers thought their mission to steal the Mona Cheesa was a "feta-compli" as they were about to be handed first prize at the Homage to Fromage competition. However, in a dramatic turn of events, their cunning disguise was unmasked by international cat of mystery, William. The furry rogues then fled the scene of the crime.

"To see the thieves go unpunished really grates,"

said Monsieur Gruyère, custodian of the Mona Cheesa.

Police urged the public to stay alert, saying the suspects, described as "small and mousy," had gone underground but were likely to strike again. "Do not underestimate these villains," warned police. "They will do almost anything to get their next cheese fix and could be hiding in a baseboard near you."

FIN